The MAGIC JOURNEY

Published in the United States by Houghton Mifflin Company, Boston.
(s04)

www.polarexpress.com
www.polarexpressmovie.com

Library of Congress Cataloging-in-Publication Data

West, Tracey, 1965–
The magic journey / by Tracey West.
p. cm.
"The Polar Express."
Based on the motion picture screenplay by Robert Zemeckis and William Broyles, Jr. ;
based on the book The Polar Express written and illustrated by Chris Van Allsburg.
Summary: A magical train ride on Christmas Eve takes a boy to the North Pole to receive a special gift from Santa Claus.
ISBN 0-618-47788-8
[1. North Pole–Fiction. 2. Santa Claus–Fiction. 3. Christmas–Fiction.]
I. Zemeckis, Robert, 1952– II. Broyles, William. III. Van Allsburg, Chris. IV. Title.
PZ7.W51937Mag 2004
[E]–dc22
2004005232

Manufactured in the United States of America
LBM 10 9 8 7 6 5 4 3 2 1

ADAPTED
BY
TRACEY WEST

BASED ON THE MOTION PICTURE SCREENPLAY
BY
ROBERT ZEMECKIS AND WILLIAM BROYLES, JR.

BASED ON THE BOOK *THE POLAR EXPRESS*, WRITTEN AND ILLUSTRATED
BY
CHRIS VAN ALLSBURG

DESIGN
BY
DOYLE PARTNERS

HOUGHTON MIFFLIN COMPANY, BOSTON 2004

YEARS AGO, ON A SNOWY CHRISTMAS EVE, A BOY LAY QUIETLY IN BED.

He was waiting—waiting for the jingle of Santa's sleigh bells on the roof.

He wanted to believe that Santa was real, but deep down, he just wasn't certain. If he heard the sound of sleigh bells and saw Santa, then he would be sure. Only then.

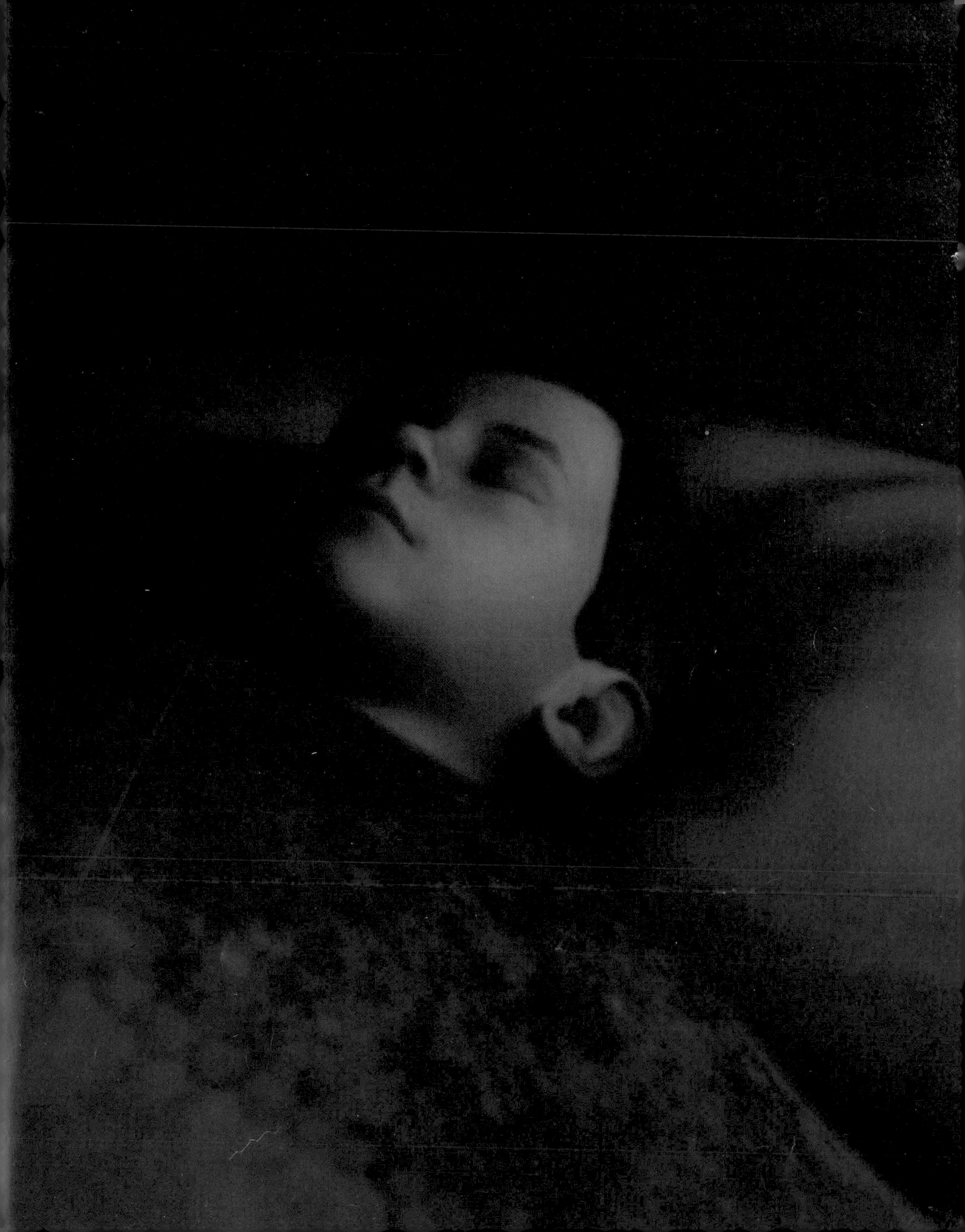

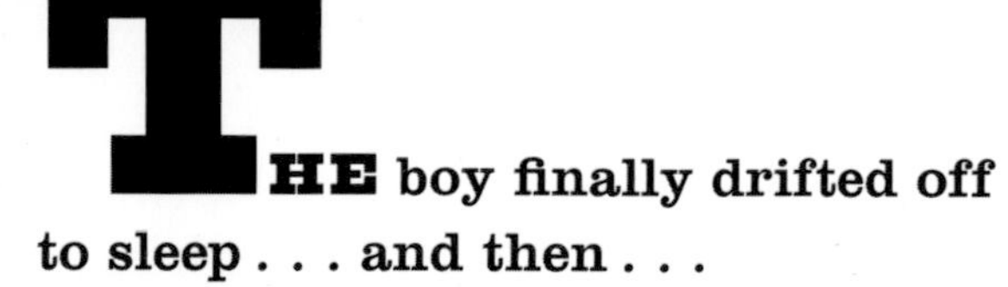

THE boy finally drifted off to sleep . . . and then . . .

A bell rang out! The boy sat up in bed and looked at his clock. It was exactly 11:55.

Suddenly, the whole house began to shake! A blinding light poured through the window, and a thunderous roar filled the air.

The boy quickly put on his robe and slippers. He ran outside to see what was causing the commotion. Was it Santa?

As the steam cleared, the boy saw a huge train sitting in front of his house.

A conductor stepped out of a passenger car. "All aboard!" he cried. "All aboard the Polar Express, bound for the North Pole!"

The boy hesitated. The North Pole? Could it really be true? There was only one way to find out. He climbed aboard.

Excited children crowded the car. As the train lurched ahead, the boy met two other passengers: a girl, and a boy who seemed to know everything.

"This train is a Baldwin 2-8-4 S3 class Berkshire-type steam locomotive," Know-It-All announced.

"It's a magic train," the girl said. "We're going to the North Pole!"

As the train pulled out of the boy's neighborhood, the Conductor came around to collect their tickets. To his surprise, the boy found one in his pocket.

The Conductor punched it, and when the boy looked at it, he saw that the Conductor's punches had formed the letters "**B**" and "**E**." Now that was strange!

AT the next stop, the train paused in front of a sad-looking house with a lonely-looking boy out front. The boy watched as the Conductor stepped out to talk to the Lonely Boy. The Conductor asked the Lonely Boy if he wanted to come aboard, but the boy shook his head no.

The Conductor sighed and got back on the train, and the wheels began to move.

Through the window, the boy could see that the Lonely Boy had changed his mind. He ran toward the train, trying to catch up.

The boy wanted to help the Lonely Boy. "Stop the train!" he yelled, but nobody heard him. So the boy did a bold thing—he pulled the emergency brake!

THE train screeched to a halt. The Lonely Boy jumped on the train but went to sit in the observation car all by himself.

When the Conductor found out what had happened, he forgave the boy for pulling the brake and ordered the waiters to bring hot chocolate to everybody. The Conductor and the girl decided to bring some to the Lonely Boy.

The boy saw that the girl had left her ticket behind—and it hadn't been punched yet. He ran between the cars to give it to her, but the wind whisked it out of his hand!

The boy felt terrible. The Conductor looked grave when he found out that the ticket had been lost.

"You'll have to come with me, young lady," he told the girl.

"HE'LL probably throw her off of the train," said Know-It-All.

The boy knew he had to save the girl, so he went to pull the emergency brake again. But just then, he spotted the girl's ticket —the wind had blown it right back into the train. Now he just had to get it back to its owner.

The Lonely Boy told him that the Conductor had taken the girl to the roof, so the boy climbed up. It was snowing hard. The boy looked for the girl, but instead found a hobo sitting in front of a roaring fire.

"I am the King of the North Pole," the hobo said. The hobo put on his skis, hoisted the boy on to his shoulders, and started to ski across the snowy roof of the train. The boy could barely see in the blizzard.

"We need to hurry!" the hobo yelled. "We have to get to the engine before we reach Flat Top Tunnel."

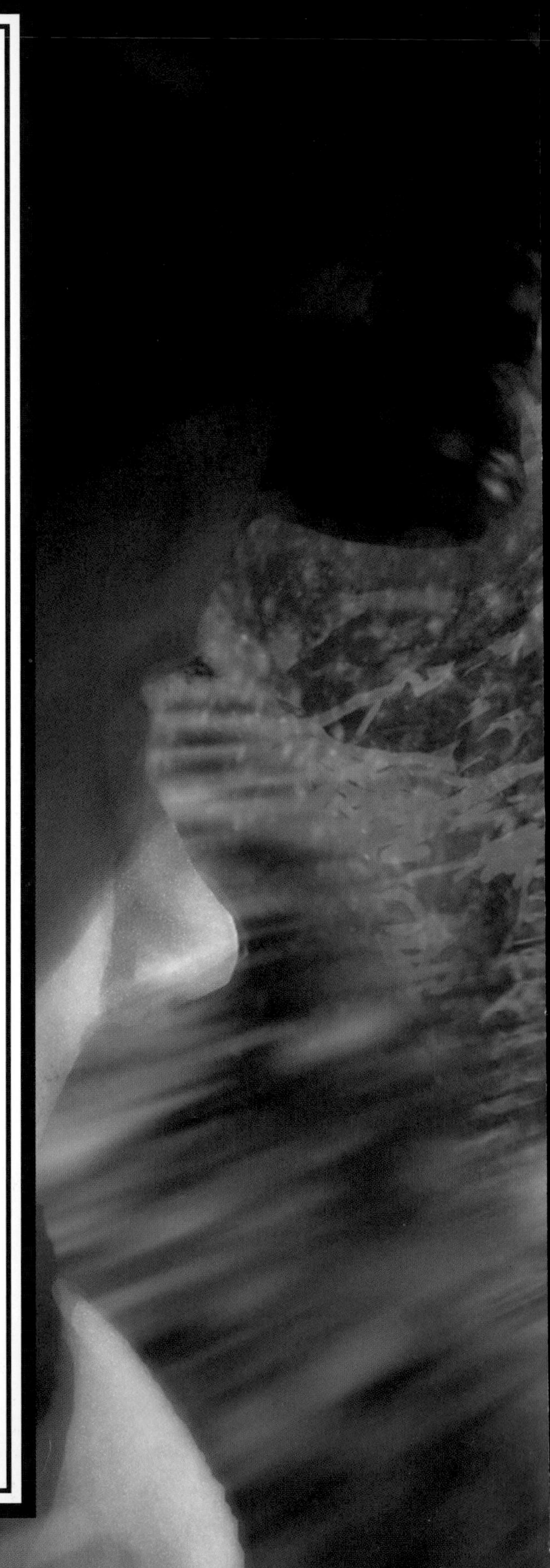

POLAR EXPRESS

THEY jumped from car to car as the tunnel got closer and closer. It looked as if they weren't going to make it, when the King yelled...

"Jump!"

The boy jumped and landed in the coal bin just in time, but the King had vanished.

The boy crawled through the coal and came out into the locomotive cab. There, the girl was sitting on the engineer's bench. She hadn't been thrown off the train after all!

"They put me in charge!" the girl announced happily. "You can help, too. Blow the whistle for me."

The boy tugged the cord, and the train whistle sang out. "I wanted to do that my whole life!" the boy shouted.

THE boy looked out the window and saw two strange men. They were changing the bulb in the headlamp on the front of the engine. “That’s Steamer the Engineer and Smokey the Fireman,” the girl whispered to the boy. “They showed me how to drive the train.”

Suddenly Steamer yelled out, “STOP THE TRAIN!”

AHEAD of the train was a massive herd of arctic caribou crossing the tracks. The girl pulled the brake just in time. When it was safe to keep going, the train charged ahead—but then a pin came loose from the brakes!

The train raced up and down the hilly track like a car on a roller-coaster ride until Steamer and Smokey fixed the brake, bringing the wild ride to a safe end.

THE Conductor and the children climbed back on top of the train and the boy gave the Conductor the girl's ticket. The Conductor punched two letters in it: "**L**" and "**E**." Then he led them back to the passenger car.

The boy and girl went looking for the Lonely Boy and found him at the rear platform of the observation car. He was softly singing a song: "*I guess that Santa's busy cause he never comes around.*"

The boy and girl realized why the Lonely Boy was so sad and lonely. He had never had a Christmas tree, or even a Christmas present.

Then the Conductor called out to them. "Look, you three. We've reached the North Pole!"

IN the distance, the sparkling lights of North Pole City came into view. As they got closer, the boy could see that Christmas lights covered every building, every bridge. The tall clock tower read exactly 11:55.

"Where are the elves?" the girl asked as the train came to a stop.

"They are gathering in the center of the city, where one of you children will receive the first gift of Christmas," answered the Conductor. "So everyone please exit the train and line up!"

THE boy and girl were at the end of the line—and then realized that the Lonely Boy had not left the train. They ran to find him, but when they climbed onto the observation car, the boy accidentally hit a lever that disconnected the car from the rest of the train!

The observation car raced backward at rapid speed. The boy tried to pull the brake, but it was too heavy. Then he felt a ghostly presence behind him, helping him stop the train. Was it the King? Before he could find out, the car stopped in a strange round room with seven tunnel exits.

WHICH tunnel do we take?" the boy asked.

"I hear a sleigh bell," the girl said, pointing to one of the tunnels. "Let's take that one."

"I hear it, too," said the Lonely Boy.

The boy couldn't hear the bell at all, but he kept silent. He followed the two friends into the tunnel.

The tunnel led them to the great gift-sorting hall.

One present whizzed by on the conveyor belt. The boy read the name and address out loud.

"Hey!" the Lonely Boy said, his voice filled with excitement. "That's MY present!"

The Lonely Boy jumped on the conveyor belt to grab the present . . . and disappeared right through a hole in the wall!

THE girl and boy jumped on to the conveyor belt after him. On the other side of the wall they all spilled out into a gigantic sack of gifts.

Suddenly the gift sack began to rise into the air. The boy looked up, and saw that it was carried by a zeppelin driven by elves.

"Let's climb up!" the girl cried.

But the Lonely Boy would not leave the sack until he found his present. And there was another surprise for them hidden in the pile of gifts —Know-It-All!

"I want to make sure I'm getting everything on my list," he said.

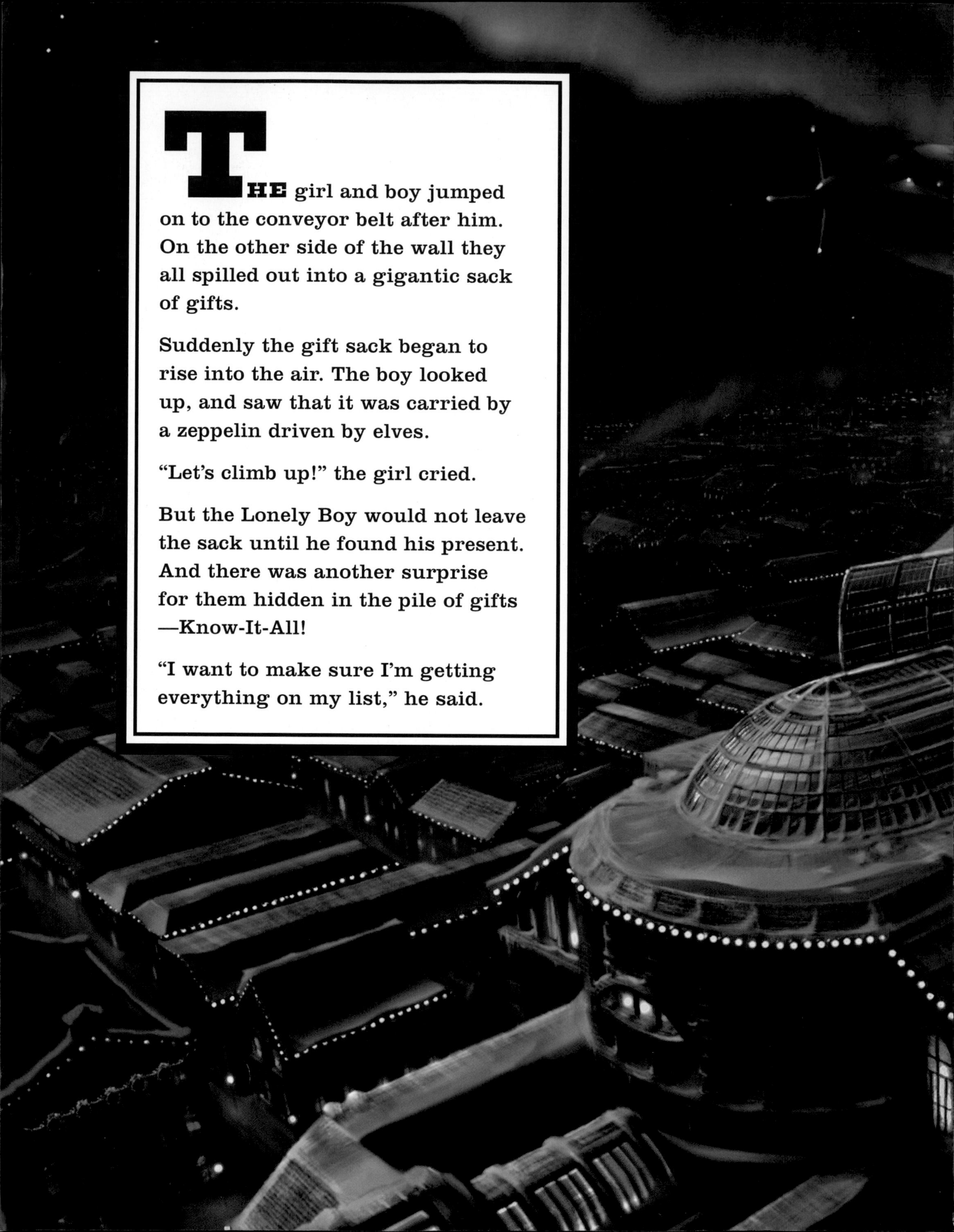

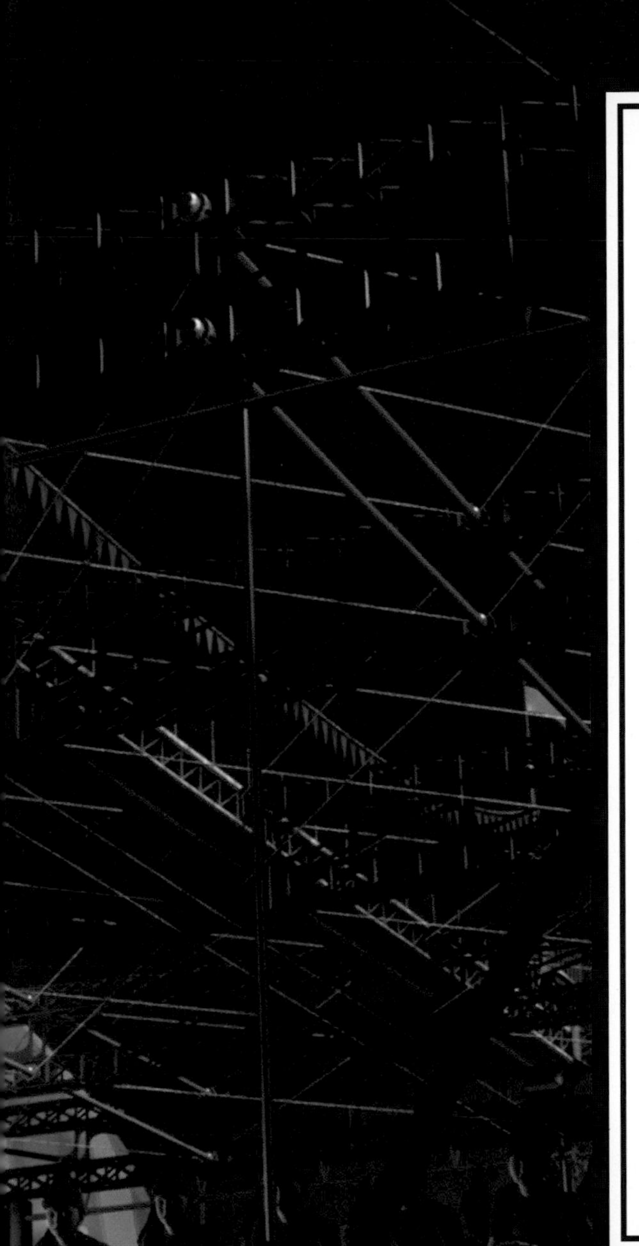

THE zeppelin sailed toward the town square. Soon it was time to descend. The elves let helium out of the zeppelin, and it sank lower and lower.

But it sank too low . . . the giant toy sack was about to crash into a Christmas tree! The elves had to act fast. Dozens of elves jumped from the zeppelin using tiny parachutes. That did the trick. The newly lightened zeppelin lifted up again, clearing the top of the tree. It made a safe landing in the square.

The boy and girl and Know-It-All slid down to safety, but the Lonely Boy still refused to leave without his present.

"Don't worry," a kindly elf told him. "It's in good hands."

THE friends joined the crowd of children waiting for Santa. The sound of trumpets filled the air, and then the elves led eight reindeer into the town square. Each of the reindeer wore a harness of bells that shook as it moved.

"Isn't that the most beautiful sound?" the girl asked.

But the boy couldn't hear the bells! *Why can't I?* he wondered.

Then the elves sang out, "*Santa Claus is coming to town!*"

"He's here! I see him!" screamed the children.

The boy couldn't see over the crowd. Was Santa really there? He felt awful. Now he would never get the proof he so desperately wanted. He would never truly believe.

SUDDENLY a bell flew off one of the harnesses. It soared through the air . . . and the boy caught it! He shook it, but heard nothing.

The boy closed his eyes. Everyone else heard the bell. Why couldn't he?

All at once he knew. They could hear the bell because they believed.

The boy thought about his amazing journey to the North Pole: the rush and roar of the train, the kindness of the Conductor, the song of the elves, the help of his new friends. All of those things were real. And if they were real, Santa must be, too.

"I believe," the boy whispered.

Ting-a-ling. The bell softly jingled —and the boy heard it.

"I believe!" the boy said to himself more confidently.

HE bell rang again, louder this time, and the boy heard every joyous sound. He opened his eyes—and saw Santa standing over him!

"What is that you said?" Santa asked.

"I . . . believe . . . this is yours," the boy stammered. He handed the bell back to Santa.

Santa smiled. "Why, thank you! Ho, ho, ho!"

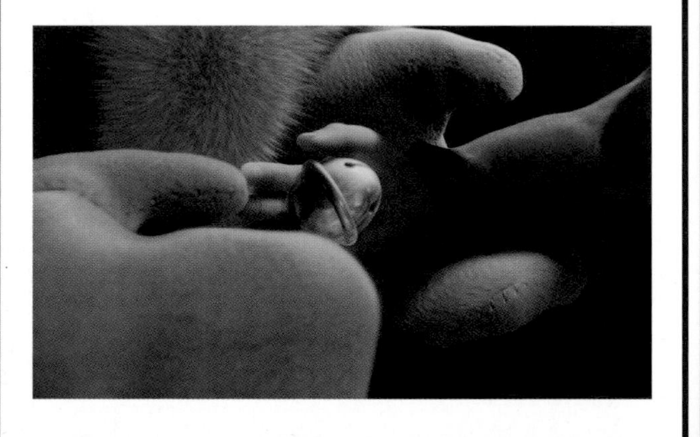

IT was time for Santa to choose the boy or girl who would receive the first gift of Christmas. He pointed right at the boy.

"Let's have this fellow right here!" Santa said.

The boy couldn't believe it. Santa asked him what he wanted, and the boy knew just the thing. He whispered in Santa's ear.

Santa smiled and handed the sleigh bell to the boy.

"The First Gift of Christmas!" Santa cried.

The boy put the bell in his pocket. Then he watched as Santa flew off in his sleigh.

CONDUCTOR

THE Conductor punched their tickets as they boarded the train again. He added more letters, and the children saw that this time, they spelled out words.

Know-It-All's ticket read **LEARN**. "There is always more to learn," the Conductor told him.

The Lonely Boy's ticket was magical. The word on it kept changing. First it read **DEPEND**. When he turned it over, it read **RELY**. Then when he flipped it over again, it read **COUNT**. The Conductor said "Because you can depend on, rely on, and count on your new friends."

The girl's ticket read **LEAD**. "I'd follow you anywhere, ma'am," the Conductor said, smiling.

The boy had a feeling about what word would be on his ticket. And he was right: **BELIEVE**.

As the train chugged away from the North Pole, the boy reached into his pocket to take out the bell. It was gone! His pocket had a hole in it. The boy felt terrible, but there was no time to look for his gift.

The train reached its first stop quickly: the house of the Lonely Boy. This time, the house didn't look so sad. A decorated Christmas tree twinkled in the front window! The Lonely Boy raced inside and came back out holding his present. Santa had delivered it after all.

The boy's stop came next. He said goodbye to his new friends. As he stepped inside his house, he saw someone else waving to him from the roof of the train—the ghost of the hobo.

The Conductor then waved and yelled to the boy, "Merry Christmas!"

HE next morning, the boy raced out of bed as soon as he woke up. There were stacks of presents under the tree, including one special present with the boy's name on it. The boy unwrapped the box. The first thing he saw was a note:

FOUND THIS ON THE SEAT OF MY SLEIGH. BETTER FIX THAT HOLE IN YOUR POCKET. MR. C.

The boy smiled. A note from Santa! And underneath, silver and shining bright, was the sleigh bell. The boy gave the bell a shake.

"Too bad," said his mom.
"It's broken."

The boy's parents couldn't hear the ring. But the boy and his sister could. They smiled at each other.

WHEN the boy grew up, he rang the bell every Christmas. And every Christmas he heard its beautiful sound, because he never stopped believing.

The bell still rings for him to this day—as it does for everyone who truly believes.